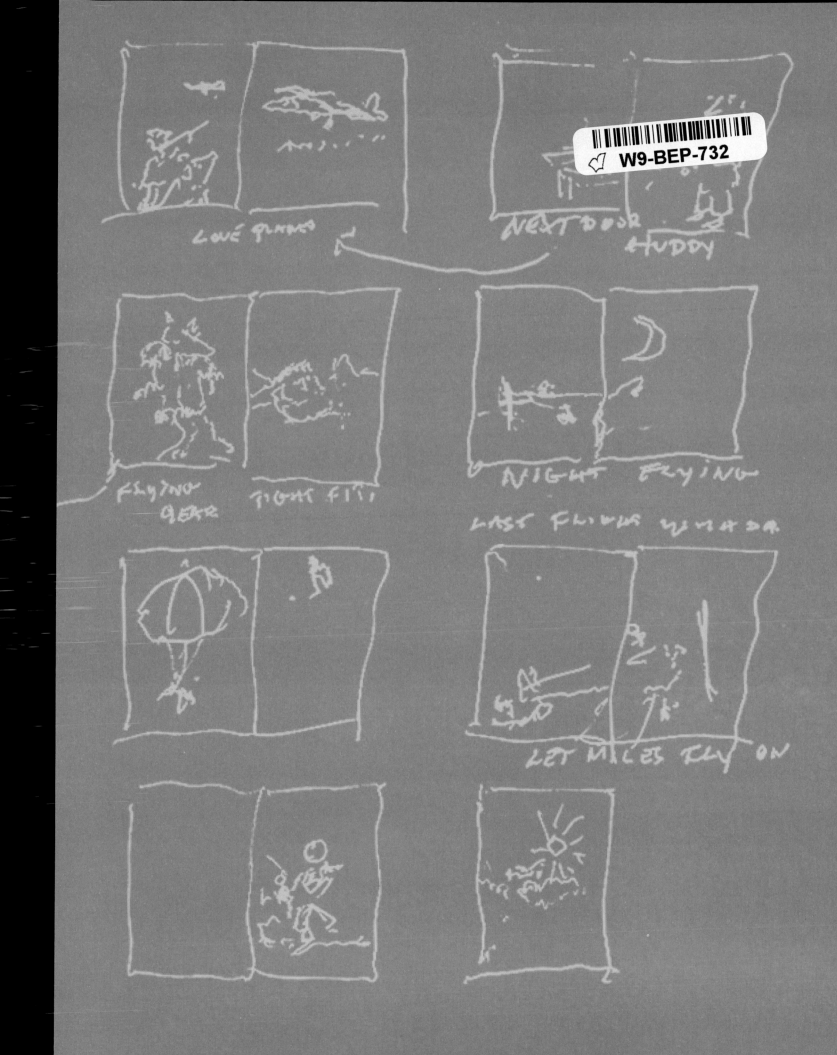

Miles, our much-loved, difficult dog

My husband, John, wrote two stories about Miles, our much-loved but very difficult Jack Russell—the first was titled Motor Miles. *While thinking about his second Miles story,* Air Miles, *John became very ill and realized he might not be able to finish this book. John asked me if I would finish* Air Miles *for him. At this point, Miles had died, so I thought my contribution could be my homage to the two much-loved men in my life.*

Illustrating Air Miles *was not easy for many reasons. John's dear friend Bill Salaman offered to write the story as far as he remembered from what John had told him. Bill wrote a very beautiful and moving version of John's story. Three of John's illustrations are also included in the book, and we have used his thumbnail sketches for the endpapers.*

Helen Oxenbury, 2021

With thanks to Gordon Grant for making Miles's plane from John's sketches

First US edition 2022
First published by Penguin Random House (UK) 2021
Library of Congress Catalog Card Number pending
ISBN 978-1-5362-2334-7

22 23 24 25 26 27 TLF 10 9 8 7 6 5 4 3 2 1

Printed in Dongguan, Guangdong, China

This book was typeset in Goudy Old Style.
The illustrations were done in pencil, watercolor, and gouache.

Candlewick Press
99 Dover Street
Somerville, Massachusetts 02144

www.candlewick.com

This is Miles.
He lives with Norman Trudge
and Norman's mother, Alice Trudge.

Miles doesn't chase
balls like he used to.

His legs hurt when
he goes for walks.

Sometimes he can't hear Norman
and Alice when they call for him.

"I think Miles needs something new
 and exciting to cheer him up,"
Alice Trudge said.

"Let's ask our neighbor
 Mr. Huddy if he can help."

Mr. Huddy had once made a car for Miles.

When he was younger, Miles drove it around the countryside, so Mr. Huddy was the right person to ask.

"I've been making an airplane," said Mr. Huddy.

"When we find a pilot who's small
   enough to fit in the cockpit,
   we can go to the field across
   the road and try it out."

"Could Miles be your pilot?" Norman asked.
"After all, he's small and can drive a car.
   Couldn't he fly your airplane as well?"

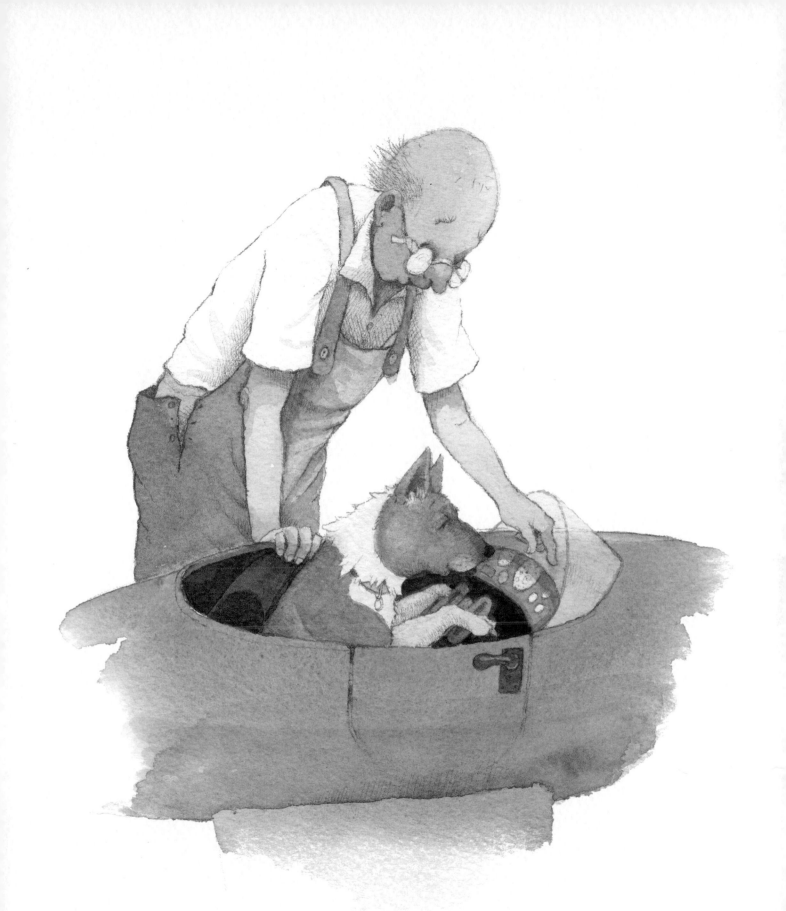

Quickly, Miles learned how to fly.

On a sunny day, with the engine roaring
and the propeller whirring, the plane sped
across the field and rose into the air.

Miles was flying.

Miles was tired when he returned.
Norman had to help him
out of the cockpit.

Miles slept for the rest of
the day.

The next time, he flew farther—
over the lakes and hills.

Along the coast.

Into the clouds.

And sometimes he flew at night . . . .

exploring the country, flying across big cities.

Each time Miles landed
in the field, Norman helped
him out of the cockpit.

Soon after, Miles stopped
wanting to go for walks.
He stopped enjoying
his food.

And he even stopped flying
his plane.

One day, Miles climbed out
of his basket in the kitchen
and left the house.

Norman followed him
to the field where the
plane was parked.

Gently, Norman lifted Miles into the cockpit.

The engine burst into life. Miles raced
over the grass, then headed for the sky.

He flew higher than ever before.

He flew farther than ever before.

HUDDY MAKING PLANE
PLANE MADE

watch take off

WAVE AT AIRLINER

Sadness.   Sad Daddy.